URSULA K. LE GUIN

JANE ON
HER OWN

A Catwings Tale

Illustrations by
S. D. SCHINDLER

ORCHARD BOOKS : NEW YORK
AN IMPRINT OF SCHOLASTIC INC.

LIBRARY OF CONGRESS CATALOGING-IN-PUBLICATION DATA AVAILABLE
ISBN 0-439-55192-7 ✦ LC No. 98030100

10 9 8 7 6 5 4 3 2 1   03 04 05 06 07

Printed in the U.S.A. 40 ✦ This edition, May 2003
The text of this book is set in 14 point CG Cloister.
The illustrations are pen-and-ink drawings and wash.

Jane on Her Own

In loving memory
of Willie and
Archie
—U.K.L.

For Spook, Fifi, and
Gladys
—S.D.S.

IT WAS A WARM AFTERNOON, and the six cats of Overhill Farm were lying about the barnyard, snoozing and talking, yawning at butterflies, purring in the sun.

Alexander Furby, who lived up at the farmhouse, came every day to visit Thelma and Roger, Harriet and James, and their little sister, Jane, who all lived in the barn loft.

It was Jane who sat up suddenly. "Thelma!" she said. "Why do we have wings?"

"We don't know, Jane," her big sister answered. "Our mother didn't have wings. Alexander doesn't. Most cats don't. We don't know why we do."

"I know why!" said Jane.

"Why?" said Thelma.

"To fly with!" Jane shouted, and she flew straight up in the air, turned two somersaults and a loop-the-loop, stalled, and crashed right on top of Alexander Furby.

Alexander was a fine, sweet cat, but rather lazy. When his dear friend Jane dived out of the air and squashed him, he just sighed and said, "Oh, Jane, don't!" And he went back to sleep, a little flatter than before.

"If we can fly," said Jane, "why do we always have to stay here in the same place and never fly anywhere and never see anything?"

Her big brother Roger said, "Oh, Jane, you know why."

Her big sister Harriet said, "Because if human beings saw cats with wings, they'd put us in cages in zoos."

Her big brother James said, "Or they'd put us in cages in laboratories."

"Being different is difficult," Thelma said. "And sometimes very dangerous."

"I know, I know," Jane said. She flew off and made faces at a woodpecker in one of the oak trees near the barn. To herself she said, "But I like difficult things, and I like dangerous things, and everything here is boring!"

She saw Hank and Susan coming over the
hill with a bag of fresh kibble. She called down
to the others, "Hank and Susan are human
beans, and they didn't put us in cages!"

"Hank and Susan are human be-ings,"

James said carefully, "but they are special ones."

Jane wasn't listening. She was flying higher and higher all by herself and singing, "Me-me-me-me-me-me-meeee!"

That was a whisper-song she had sung to herself when she was a tiny kitten. Her mother had been chased away from her. Jane had hidden all alone in an attic full of hungry, angry rats. Here on the farm she didn't think about that terrible time anymore. But when she was unhappy, she sang her old song, "Me-me-me-me-me-me-meeee!"

She was unhappy now because everything was always the same, and everybody was always the same, and she wanted to see new places and find new friends. If her brothers and sisters and Alexander were all content to stay here, well, they could stay here, but she was going to stretch her wings.

The next morning she did just that. She flew up over the barn roof, and the wind was so sweet and fresh that she knew it was time to go. Alexander was just coming over the hill. She swooped down and kissed his pink nose. "Good-bye. I'm going adventuring!" she called. And off she flew above the forest and the hills.

"Alexander will miss me," she thought. But she knew that he would get over it, if he had plenty to eat. "And I will miss them all," she thought. But she knew that she would get over it, because there were adventures waiting, and the wind was blowing, and she was on the wing.

2

JANE FLEW OVER FARMS AND
TOWNS. She hunted for her food in wild
places and slept up in trees in the woods, for
she soon found that the farms and towns were
not friendly. If she flew out of the sky at cats
without wings, they hissed and spat and tried
to scratch her or catch her. They didn't real-
ize she was a cat and were scared of her. If
she flew out of the sky at human beings, first
they screamed, and then they shouted, "What
is it? What is it? Catch it! Catch it!" And that
scared Jane. If she flew out of the sky at dogs,
they jumped and barked until their eyes
crossed. That was fun. But nowhere could she
find a friend.

Did having wings mean she had to be lonely?
Birds had wings, of course, but very few birds
would even say anything polite to a winged cat.
And owls and hawks were dangerous.

But one day Jane and a crow lighted on
the same branch. They looked a little bit alike,
and the crow was not at all afraid of Jane.
He winked at her. "Hey, you!" he said. "Cat

with wings! You ought to be on TV!" And
he flew off, going "Caw! Caw! Caw!"

Jane thought she knew what TV was: big
dishes outside farmhouses and metal poles
on top of apartment houses in the city. She
didn't know why she ought to be on dishes
or on poles. But she thought about the city
where she had been born. She remembered

the exciting smells and noises. "Maybe in the city I can find a friend!" she thought.

She was tired and very hungry when she came to the city. It was a hot summer evening. The rooftops seemed to go on and on forever. She flew over them, wondering where to find food and water. An apartment window stood wide open, as if inviting her. "Here goes!" thought Jane. And she flew right in.

There was one human being in the room. He was short and rather plump, like Alexander. First he screamed a little, but Jane was used to that. Then he stared at her. He didn't try to catch her. He just stared at her, with eyes as round as fishes' eyes.

"Prrr, prrr, me-me-me," sang Jane, flying around the room. She brushed the man's nose with her silky black tail and patted his head with her soft paw as she flew by.

"Oh you bee-yoo-tee-full A-MA-ZING whatever-you-are!" said the man. And when

she flew past again, he held out his hand, but he didn't try to catch her.

Then he hurried to the dish cupboard and the refrigerator, and poured a bowl full of milk, and put it on the table.

"Prrrooo!" cried Jane, and dived straight into it, for she was famished.

The man went and closed the window. She did not notice, being busy drinking and then washing. Her mother, Mrs. Jane Tabby, had taught her always to wash after meals. The man just sat and watched her. He kept saying, "You are so amazing! You are so terrific! Oh, Baby, thank you for flying into my life!" He had a nice voice, and when he said, "Hey, Baby, will you come to Poppa?" Jane walked across the table to him and said, "Me?"

He petted her. She flattened out at first. But he had gentle hands, and Jane was very tired and very full of milk. She climbed onto his lap, folded her wings, curled up, purred a little, and fell asleep.

"Oh you beautiful Baby," said the man. "Do I have plans for you!"

And the next day Jane began to find out what his plans were.

3

JANE WISHED Thelma and Roger and Harriet and James could see how well Poppa treated her. No cages! No zoos! No laboratories! Of course the window stayed closed. But Poppa petted her and admired her and gave her the most delicious food. He got her a special soft bed with silk curtains and a cat carrier lined with purple velvet and furnished with catnip mice. People came every day to see her, or she went in her cat carrier to meet them. All of them praised and admired her. Even Alexander had never been spoiled the way Poppa spoiled her!

Poppa always called her Baby when they were alone. But when the people came to see

her, men with briefcases and men with cameras, he would say, "And now, I present—MISS MYSTERY!" He would open the door of the cat carrier, and Jane would walk out with her tail in the air. She would sit down and look around, and perhaps wash one paw a little. And then—then—she would open her wings and fly up into the air. All the men would stare, and their mouths would fall open, and when she loop-the-looped, they all said, "Ooooooh!"

Then they would talk with Poppa, while Jane circled the light fixtures or swooped down to Poppa's shoulder and sat and washed his ear. She was fond of him, for he was always kind. But she didn't much like the briefcase men. They always looked at her once and then began talking to one another very fast and never looked at her again. And the cameramen wanted her to do stupid things. She would have liked to show them how she could hunt, out in the open fields, as fast as any falcon. But they held up silly hoops with paper on them and expected her to fly through them. She would have liked to fly around the city having adventures, but they wanted her to stay inside and do tricks. And the eyes of their cameras watched her and watched her, like the eyes of owls.

Poppa showed her a picture in a newspaper. "See, Baby?" he said, petting her. "That's you! That's my beautiful amazing Baby!" But pictures that didn't move didn't interest Jane.

Only when Poppa showed her his TV set did she remember what the crow had said: "You ought to be on TV!" Poppa put in a videocassette and said, "Now watch this, Baby honey!" She looked, and she saw a cat with wings, flying.

"Harriet!" she cried. "James!"

But it was a black cat.

"Me," Jane said sadly. And she sat and watched herself catching catnip mice in the air and flying through hoops.

"Baby, you're going to be the biggest thing since cornflakes," Poppa said, and tickled her behind the ears. "Miss Mystery, the Cat with Wings!"

"Prr," Jane said. But her heart was troubled.

"Come on, Baby, eat your dinner," Poppa said. "Tuna fish with cream for Miss Mystery!"

But Jane wasn't hungry. She got no exercise except when she was flying for the cameramen. She never was in the open air. Wherever she and Poppa went, he carried her in her elegant cat carrier. In all the rooms she was in, the windows were always tightly closed. And the purple silk ribbon she had to wear made her feel as if she were choking. She didn't want to eat.

She flew over to the window, stood on the sill with her front paws on the glass, and looked out at the busy city street. She couldn't hear the noises; she couldn't smell the smells. She looked at Poppa and mewed very sadly.

"Baby honey, I can't let you out," he said.

"You know that! It's dangerous out there!"

He petted her. He offered her cat candy.
Jane nearly bit him.

"This is worse than the farm!" she thought.

4

WHEN THEY BEGAN GOING every
day to what Poppa called the Studio, it got
even worse.

The Studio was a huge room with black
walls and no windows at all. It was full of briefcase men, and cameramen with their cameras,
and electric cords like snakes, and hot, glar-
ing lights. She had to wear the nasty purple
ribbon all the time. She had to do tricks and
fly through imitation windows. They kept
trying to make her eat a kind of kibble she
didn't like at all. And everything she did,
she had to do over and over. And the men got
cross and shouted, and the camera eyes turned,
watching her like owls, wherever she flew.

"You're a TV star, Baby! You're Miss Mystery!" Poppa told her when she got tired and nervous. "Everybody's going to love you! Everybody's going to know you!"

That made Jane think.

"If everybody knows there is one cat with wings," she thought, "maybe they'll go looking for more catwings. And maybe they'll find Overhill Farm. And maybe they'll capture Roger and Thelma and James and Harriet, and make them wear purple ribbons and fly through hoops! Oh, what have I done?"

She made up her mind then that she must escape. She didn't want to disappoint Poppa, but she thought he'd get over it. So she ate all her fine dinner that night, for strength. And then she waited. Cats are good at waiting.

Since the evening she flew into his life, Poppa had never opened the window of his apartment even a crack. He knew she would fly out if she could. But thinking about her wings, he forgot that she had four paws.

He stood in the doorway, shaking hands and saying good-bye to two of the briefcase

men. They were saying, "Millions of dollars!" and Poppa was listening happily. None of them noticed the little black shadow that slipped past their legs. Paw by paw, it followed the briefcase men down the stairs. When they opened the street door, the little black shadow darted out, flew up into the night air, and was gone.

Oh, the wonderful cool wind on her wings, and the wonderful roaring, crashing, yowling noises of the city streets, and the wonderful, awful city smells! "I'm free, me, me, I'm free!" Jane sang out loud, flying high. And she flew on all night, singing.

When the morning came, she lighted on a roof, hid under a chimney, and slept all day. She had learned her lesson. No more flying in the daylight and no more flying in any window she didn't know!

At evening she woke to find a pigeon staring at her.

"Roo-roo, who are you?" it asked.

"I am Miss Mystery!" Jane shouted and jumped at the pigeon to scare it.

It wasn't very scared. "Some necktie you got," it said and waddled off.

Jane realized that the purple silk ribbon was still tied around her neck. She tried to claw it off, but she had tried that before. Nothing she could do would make it come loose. She sat on the roof as the sun set and asked herself, "Where do I go now?"

5

SHE ANSWERED HERSELF, "I'll go see Mother!"

James had told her about the Homing Instinct of cats, and her Homing Instinct told her that this was the wrong part of the city. Where she had been born, the buildings were smaller and older, and in the streets there weren't so many car roofs, and more tops of people's heads. She leaped up into the air and flew.

It was a long way, but as day was breaking, she found a big park where she could drink from a fountain. And soon after that she came to the street where her mother lived. She flew straight to the rooftop where a little house stood in a roof garden of plants in pots.

It was a warm autumn dawn. The door of the little roof house was shut, but a window was partway open. Jane squeezed in.

It was dark inside, but she heard purring. She followed the purring and found a bed.

Somebody was sleeping soundly in the bed, and curled up on the covers was Jane's mother, purring.

"Mother! It's Me!"

"Who is that?" cried Mrs. Tabby, startled.

"Me! Jane!"

"Oh, my dear kitten!" said Mrs. Tabby. She immediately began to wash Jane's ears. She and Jane purred madly and talked in whispers. "Wherever have you been, my dear?"

"I got bored on the farm and went to a city," Jane explained. "But you were right, Mother! Human beans do catch catwings and put them in cages!"

"Well, some of them do, and some of them don't," said Mrs. Tabby. "If you want to stay, I think we can trust my friend here."

"She certainly is comfortable," said tired Jane, snuggling up against the warm old woman in the bed.

"And kind," said Mrs. Tabby.

So when the old woman, whose name was Sarah Wolf, woke up next morning, she found her old friend Mrs. Jane Tabby curled up on one side of her legs—and on the other side was a black cat she had never seen before, sound asleep.

"Well, hello," said Sarah Wolf. "Aren't you pretty!"

Jane woke up, yawned, and said, "Me?"

Then she stood up and stretched her legs and her wings, one by one.

"My goodness!" said Sarah Wolf.

Very gently she reached out to let Jane sniff her fingers. Very gently she scratched Jane's cheeks and stroked Jane's silky wings.

"How beautiful!" she said. "There weren't any cats with wings when I was young. At least I don't remember any. But things keep changing. And it seems a very good idea. Although if I were a bird, I might not think so. And I expect it might be wise not to tell people about you. They'd just say, 'Oh, Sarah is so old, she's gone silly. Now she's seeing cats with wings!' It's difficult being different, isn't it?"

Mrs. Jane Tabby sat up and stretched.

"Mrs. Jane," said Sarah Wolf, "is this a friend of yours?"

The two cats leaned on each other and purred.

"Why, she might be your daughter," said Sarah. "So is this Little Jane? Are you hungry, Little Jane?"

Both cats leaped off the bed and went to the empty cat dish.

But they both watched Sarah Wolf anxiously.
Would she close the window?

Sarah went to the window.

"Oh, no!" Jane thought.

Sarah opened the window wider. "I expect
that's how you'd like it," she said to Jane.

Jane flew up and landed on Sarah's shoulder and kissed her ear. "I love you!" she said.

Mrs. Tabby tangled herself around Sarah's legs, purring. "I love you," she said.

Sarah untied the purple ribbon from Jane's neck and put it in the trash. "You certainly don't need that to be beautiful," she said.

SO JANE LIVES now in the city with her mother and her friend Sarah on the rooftop with the flowerpots. All day she sleeps among the geraniums, or sits and watches the streets and skies.

Sometimes, looking westward in the early morning, she sees her brothers and sisters flying in for a visit. "How is Alexander?" she asks them, and they say, "Very fine, and rather fat." Sometimes Jane flies back to Overhill Farm with them and has long, long talks with Alexander. For she never could talk at all until he showed her that she could, and she loves Alexander.

But she always flies back to the city, because that is where she belongs. "I am an Alley Cat!" she says. "I am Miss Mystery, the Flying Black Shadow of the City Night! Beware of me! For I am Jane, and I am free! Me, me, I am free!"

And singing her song out loud, she flies through the streets and alleys every night, teasing dogs and scaring rats, finding new friends and new adventures. Sometimes as Jane flies

past a window, she hovers in the air a moment,
looking in. Through the dreams of a child
sleeping in that room flies a cat with wings,
and the child reaches out to pet it. But the
dream passes, and Jane flies on, singing her
wild catwing song.